I Can't Sleep

ISBN 1 85854 377 0
Published by Brimax Books Ltd, Newmarket, England, CB8 7AU 1996.
Second reprint 1996.
Printed in China.

I Can't Sleep

BY GILL DAVIES

Illustrated by Eric Kincaid

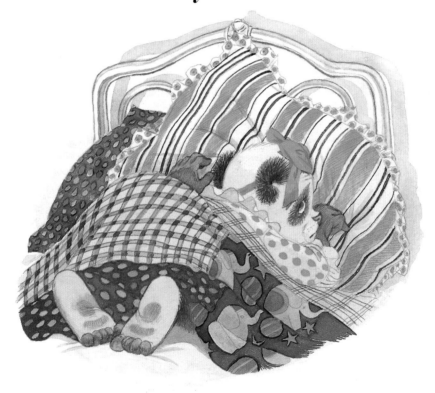

BRIMAX

Polly Panda was wide awake. She tossed and turned.
She rolled over from one side to the other.
She lay on her back. She lay on her tummy.

Finally Polly sat up and called to her mother.
"I can't sleep," said Polly.
Mrs Panda fluffed up the pillows and she tucked in the covers.

"Close your eyes and try counting sheep," said Mrs Panda.
Polly closed her eyes. She counted sheep.

One, two, three sheep - coming up the lane;
Four, five, six sheep - running back again;
Seven, eight, nine sheep - riding in a train.

"I still can't sleep," said Polly.

"Just shut your eyes and try counting elephants instead,"
said Mr Panda.
Polly closed her eyes. She counted elephants.

One, two, three elephants - in a circus show;
Four, five, six elephants - dancing to and fro;
Seven, eight, nine elephants - learning how to row.

But still Polly could not sleep.

"Try tigers," said Polly's brother, Ned. Ned liked tigers.
Polly closed her eyes. She counted tigers.

One, two, three tigers - going for a prowl;
Four, five, six tigers - like to sit and scowl;
Seven, eight, nine tigers - roar and snarl and growl.

"I think the tigers are waking me up," said Polly.

"Perhaps fish might do the trick," said Grandfather.
Polly closed her eyes. She counted fish.

One, two, three fish - swimming in a race;
Four, five, six fish - pull a funny face;
Seven, eight, nine fish - find a frog to chase.

"I'm still wide awake," said Polly.

"Shut your eyes tight and try counting pigs,"
said Grandmother Panda.
Polly closed her eyes. She counted pigs.

One, two, three pigs - playing in a sty;
Four, five, six pigs - flying in the sky;
Seven, eight, nine pigs - baking apple pie.

"Pigs don't work either," said Polly.

"When I can't sleep, I count hippos," said Uncle Fred.
Polly closed her eyes. She counted hippos.

One, two, three hippos - have a muddy wallow;
Four, five, six hippos - other hippos follow;
Seven, eight, nine hippos - open mouths to swallow.

"Hippos are very wet," said Polly yawning.

"Why don't you just count us?" said Mrs Panda,
Mr Panda, Ned, Grandfather, Grandmother
and Uncle Fred.
This time Polly kept her eyes open. She counted pandas.

Mrs Panda, Mr Panda, her bigger brother Ned,
Grandfather, Grandmother and her Uncle Fred.

Polly's eyes began to close.

"Counting pandas makes me feel very tired,"
mumbled Polly sleepily.
She could not keep her eyes open at all now.
Polly snuggled her head into the pillow.
She cuddled her teddy.

At last! Polly fell sound asleep and dreamed of...

One, two, three teddies - busy as a bee;
Four, five, six teddies - paddling in the sea;
Seven, eight, nine teddies - climbing up a tree.

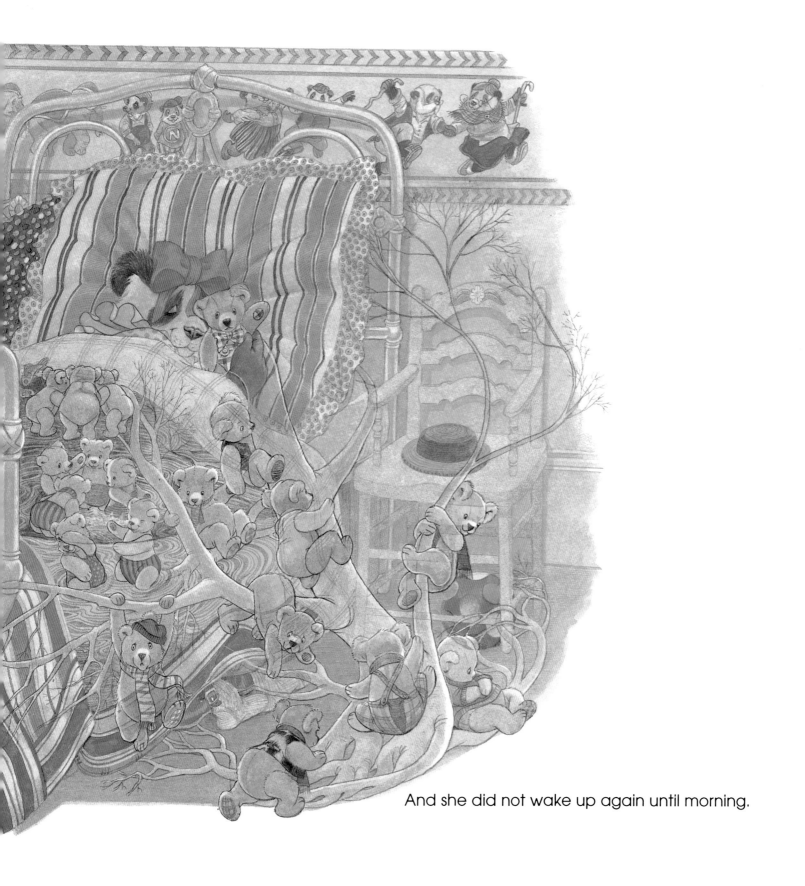

And she did not wake up again until morning.